VÉZELAY
A SENTIMENTAL GUIDE

Pour Tom,
Avec toute notre affection
Nicole & Larry
6 Août 2004.

Jules ROY

VÉZELAY
A SENTIMENTAL GUIDE

Translated from the French by Georges MICHEL,
Nicole *and* Larry MALLET

Photographs by Gérald

L'OR DES ÉTOILES

Today, one goes to Vézelay as towards a star.

For this to happen, Vézelay, already so unique on account of its geographical situation which makes it a sort of promontory pointing towards the sky, Vézelay had to receive something of great importance, and the veneration of the god who took possession of it had to have a marvel of a temple. That was not enough.

Kings had also to kneel in front of a woman, symbol of love, and that woman had to be the first witness of Christ's resurrection. Immense demonstrations of religious faith, close to fanaticism, had to find here the sign of the word which sent them blindly towards the East, to liberate Christ's tomb from the hands of the Infidels.

Abbeys, bishops, Counts of Nevers and Autun had to quarrel and tear one another apart here, Popes had to arbitrate conflicts and authenticate relics. An uncontrollable impetus had to push crowds towards the remains of this woman, and what a woman ! One of the most beautiful love-givers in all human history, but on whom monks have bestowed a severe look.

Hatred, and deadly jealousies, had to exist between denominations of the same faith ; blood had to be shed in the streets of Vézelay. People had to slay one another, the town had to be conquered and reconquered during Wars of Religion. People had to be massacred there, and had to dream of a republic. The abbey-church was saved from destruction, during the Revolution, by becoming the temple of Reason, and Vézelay almost fell into ruin until the 19th century, when a famous writer and an architect of genius rescued it from darkness.

Let's move on.

Here is Vézelay resurrected. Here is Lazarus rising from his tomb. Here are the crowds taken in once again by the magic.

Here is a star shining over Vézelay.

From the North...

One usually arrives from the North, leaving highway A6 at Nitry. Then, route D944 for 5 kilometres, and, on the outskirts of Joux-la-Ville, route D32 which passes at some distance from a prison hidden from sight, then cuts across a dry, deserted plateau with its black furrows in winter, and with its blond wheat and corn in summer. In June, there is a scent of honey on the wind. After a few hairpin turns in the road, one arrives abruptly at Voutenay, whose steeple seems to stagger. One meets the track of the local railway that links Auxerre, the city of Marie Noël, with Autun, the city of Talleyrand, then the dreadful Nationale 6 for four kilometres only. One has hardly the time to admire the languid valley of the Cure river before one perceives, far off, the towers of Vézelay. Here is the turn off, now well marked, of route D951. Another nine kilometres, and we reach the old dignified village of Asquins, whose cellars reek of old wine vats and on a steep rock, by day, looms a gloomy, threatening fortress. You will be there in three minutes.

Floodlit by night, Vézelay resembles the collar-piece of the Annonciade order. We have arrived.

Vézelay, chief town of a canton in the district of Avallon, in the Yonne department, county town Auxerre ; region of Burgundy, county town Dijon. Altitude 300 metres. Paris, 220 km ; Dijon, 120 km. 500 inhabitants, 350 voting members, including the hamlets. Railway station : Sermizelles. Postal code 89450. Saint Bernard preached the Second Crusade there. The ruins of an abbey. A famous Romanesque church. Vaulted cellars and cisterns with sculptured pillars. Homeland of Théodore de Bèze. Worldwide heritage. National historical monument. This is what you'll find in an ordinary guide-book.

Formerly, a drawbridge cut off *porte Saint-Etienne* (Saint-Stephen's gate) from *place du Barle*, which means « fortified enclosure ». Once a month, it was the cattle fair, and the place resounded with all sorts of noises, bleating, lowing, neighing. Today, from Palm Sunday to All Souls' Day, it is pilgrims' fair. Leave your car where the sign tells you. Wait for your friends if they come from elsewhere. Hotels and inns are not lacking.

Neither are policemen. Ours are friendly.

You smash into a foamy sea...

From Avallon, by route D957, it is straight ahead. A rapid descent towards the river Cousin which trickles down from the Morvan range, iridescent with flashes of iron and trout ; meadows where graze peaceful cattle as far as spot height 318, where suddenly you smash into a foaming sea.

Slow down.

Look for our hill where houses huddle together like a herd at dusk. Our towers are plumed with vapours, valleys open everywhere, intermingle, follow each other, surging like a sea of blurry outlines which resemble Tuscany or limestone formations in China. If you have good eyesight and a feel for the terrain, you will be able to discover along the Cousin the remains of the ancient Roman road, the *via Agrippa*, which came from Milan through Lyons then turned North through the Yonne valley.

There, disencumbered of everything, except for the mists which add to the feeling of vastness, you are alone. Stop. Even if you are not a believer, you will hear a cry from the very depth of your soul. *Montjoie* : « mount of joy ».

As almost everywhere in the neighbourhood, a calvary. Not in wrought iron, but in grey and pink limestone, like that of the basilica which came from here, to be precise from the village of Tharoiseau which looks like a balcony

hanging over a precipice. For the knights-errant of Lorraine and countries beyond the Rhine, if there are still any, this spot height 318 was the end of the journey, the point where mystical love brought them. Centuries ago, after so much wandering and so many nights spent in ditches, Vézelay appeared to them as close as a mortar shot, a grand monument which sheltered the shrine containing the relics of saint Magdalene : the lips which had kissed the feet of the Lord, the hair which had wiped them, that kings of France came to stroke with timid fingers.

Around the autumn or the spring equinox, if you are lucky enough to be there towards the end of the afternoon, at sunset, you will see the sun declining in the glowing incandescence of a forge and, suddenly, sinking into Vézelay. It seems as though, crossing the church, it set it on fire, and rested its fire globe on it for a moment. Perhaps this is why during Greek and Roman times so many temples to Mercury, Bacchus, Janus and other pagan gods had been erected there, then to the God of Christendom, to the One God in three persons. It is from there that, on Easter Day, March 31,1146, when it was almost snowing, the Second Crusade left with the cry of « God wills it », repeated since the First Crusade and for other motives by so many ayatollahs of all creeds. Then, drive down to Saint-Père, until you hit the foot of our rock. If you raise your eyes, you will discern a piece of grey cliff, vineyards, woods, a few dilapidated walls, a crumbling redan. Already, a vague feeling of unease, a sort of excitement mingled with a strange awareness, maybe like the awakening of love, will begin to pervade you, without your even noticing it.

If you come from the south...

From the South, the marvel appears sooner, twenty kilometres away, from the glacis of the castle of Bazoches where Vauban and his staff worked, with corner tower, watch towers, loop-holes, battlements and barbicans. D958 coming from Nevers by a charming route, is lined with hillocks which remind one of sepulchral mounds of the Gallic Wars or King Arthur's quest for the Holy Grail. Apart from that nothing but dashing mansions, points of view, vast expanses stretching to infinity. In the same way, if you arrive from Quarré-les-Tombes by route D36, then from the stronghold of Chastellux, you will be able to see more and more clearly, at each bump in the road, the amorous ladies, for you are not heading towards only one, for more than one is awaiting you. Our hill seems suspended in the sky. From the South as from the East, all roads meet at Saint-Père, at the foot of a steeple which goldsmiths have chiselled in white stone from the 11th to the 13th century. There, a tempter points out to you the three stars of the master of the restaurant *L'Espérance*.

A divine surprise

From Auxerre to the North, and past Vincelles, if you leave Nationale 6 for D950, on the right towards the West, it will be a divine surprise. There, nothing prepares you for Vézelay, except the desire to see it, certainly not the narrow gorges, the masses of fallen proud rocks where a church happens to be perched. Looking at the road signs, distance seems to shrink, the hairpin turns diminish, the ravines level out, and suddenly… It is even better if, leaving the Nevers Canal at Châtel-Censoir, you rejoin D100 then D76, long sunken thoroughfares leading, always through the West, to Asnières-sous-Bois, where, not so long ago, people used to go in order to buy wheat-flavoured bread. Don't lose hope, persevere. After the hamlet of Bois-de-la-Madeleine, a last turn and you plunge on to what grips and submerges you on the other side, hardly an angel's stride away. Try to get there by late afternoon, hold your impatience in check, keep the enthusiasm which projects you, gaping, to what ? The admirable, unexpected discovery, the sinuous hill of the Scorpio. A shining head, a body covered with a scaly membrane, a half hidden tail, roofs fitted like scales, a clock-tower, fortifications which end here and, at the very top, under a canopy of silver and azure holding, one would say, the sky, our glowing Magdalene.

Perhaps you will distinguish among the sparks of a huge black and silver diamond, a swarm of pilgrims with pink, blue, red or green parasols, climbing without really knowing why, as though towards the moon, if the moon had been promised to them. As for the holy princess, who is only alluded to, she is there. So is the moon.

Whether through the winding road on one side or the other, here you are once again at *place du Barle,* with its grand hotel which, during World War II, served as *Kommandantur* (local nazi headquarters), and others : the *Morvan*, the *Compostelle* and the *Cheval Blanc* (White Horse), where slept so many famous guests, such as Zervos, Paul Eluard, Jean Follain, Fernand Léger, Le Corbusier, and, above all, Ysé, the embodiment of love according to Claudel. All you need now is to climb straight ahead by the only

street that opens up here, and bears the name of Saint-Stephen's church, now secularized and serving as an artist's workshop. A bakery, shops, restaurants. The post-office is there, the tax-collector opposite, then Burgundy wine-sellers, groceries, bazar, pharmacy, antiques called *Le Bleu du ciel*★, photos and religious artifacts called *L'Or des Etoiles*. The tavern where Viollet-le-Duc used to play billiards has disappeared ; a carpenter has been replaced by the constabulary, now moved outside the walls. Cellars are hidden behind shutters that flap down to the ground. On the walls of dwellings where some noteworthy event took place, there is sometimes a plaque. There lived a poet, a famous heretic, a musician, a painter. The plaque on the house called *des Colombs*, from the 16th century, does not mention the name of Henri Petit, who wrote sublime pages on Vézelay, and invited there Louis Guilloux, as humble and great as he was. In literature as elsewhere, things are not always as you expect them to be. There you can read : « *Like a turtle-dove* (*colombe* in French) *humble and simple shall I be...* »

The Big Well, begun by the Romans and never completed by the monks, of considerable depth, is nowadays filled in by rubbish and perhaps a few carcasses of rebels and desperadoes. Here formerly stood one of the twelve gallows of the town, a token of the power and the justice of the abbey. It now resounds with the clinking of glasses. If you are curious, you will discover, in the upper part of the town, *rue du Tripot* (Gambling-joint street), or, in the lower town, in *rue Saint-Etienne* (Saint-Stephen's street) the heart and the pearl carved into the stone above the door, signalling that it was a house of pleasure. The old tower of Saint-Peter's church, recently struck by lightning, has burnt down once more. Its restored clock has become automatic, electronic, striking or not striking every quarter

★ Today *l'Âme Enchantée* (Publisher's note).

of an hour and twice in the hour, according to the fancy of some. Behind windows decked with pots of geraniums, or chintz curtains, people watch you as you look down the narrow windows of cellars with pink limestone pillars, where the pilgrims used to sleep. Saint-Stephen's street ends here, and goes on as Saint-Peter's street, whereas on the left the street divides : *rue de la porte-Neuve* (Newgate street) goes down hill towards the ramparts, and *rue des Ecoles* (School street) goes up hill.

It's for life...

One does not visit Vézelay the way one visits the Gioconda, in passing. If looking at the face of Mona Lisa, who served as a model for Leonardo da Vinci, you fall suddenly in love, it does not last. Here, where our fair lady is but roughly represented on the façade of the church, in the crypt and in the carved-stone museum, things are different : you fall in love for life. Yet she is not arousing as she is in the paintings by Georges de La Tour, and, still more, by Jean-Jacques Henner : her name is on all the roads that lead to her. Woods and hills belong to her. Walk at random along little local roads where no one will bother you, with the exception of a tractor carrying manure to the fields. Here and there, in openings and when you least expect it, our promontory and its ramparts will appear as Jerusalem once appeared to our fathers, glowing, blurry, then fading behind a shoulder of lucern or rapeseed, or else the branch of a fir-tree, or a hedge of hawthorn or wild rose.

To the North, leave the poorly marked paths like the one that leads to *Nobleterre* (Noble land), *Buisson chrétien* (Christian Bush) or *Champs du Genèvre* (Juniper Fields). You will only find these names on topographic map N° 2722 on a scale of 1/25,000 sold in newspaper-bookstores of the region. One kilometre West of Vézelay, you will also discover the *Goulotte*, then the state forest of *Chauffour*, and there, at spot height 275, a path full of ruts leading to the *Ruelles, Bois de Brûlis* and *Vieille Borde*, across a desolate plateau where sometimes graze, without their shepherd, sheep who know very well where they go.

If you proceed farther on, wondering who might well live there nowadays, you may come across a few ostriches in an enclosure, protected by mastiffs. Slightly uneasy, you will retrace your steps and our fatal beauty will appear to you on the other side of a valley with neither river nor stream, where waters ravage any way they want to during rainstorms. In a cul-de-sac appropriatedly called la *Bouillère* (Boiling Cauldron), if you find someone, you will finally be shown the place where lepers used to live. Vézelay is on the other side of the hill, with Magdalene's, dark and gloomy from top to bottom of its ridge. Behold her once more, ask yourself why you are on a tiny azure planet in the solar system, a minuscule part of the Milky Way, our galaxy.

Do not go too quickly...

Do not go too quickly, even on foot. If necessary, let yourself be submerged, infinitely, by a surge of hairy ears of corn or by an enormous flow of big round flowers smelling of vanilla. A stubborn shred of mist clings to the bottom of the rock. Another calvary, recently raised, is

called Mass cross or Compostella cross. Above you stand the ramparts, the walls of the transept of the basilica, like the protruding part of a fortress, with a redan pierced with cannon-holes, and the noble line of the chapter houses, with their gardens of zinnias, peonies and roses, their oak-pannelled sitting-rooms and Louis XV fireplaces, where lived a few canons, happy capons. A long time ago, after the monks were dispersed, they left us.

You are already caught and captured. What remains for you is the softest and perhaps the most loving. From the village of Asquins, where people still have a far-off memory of water corvées and barrels of wine that had to be carried up in sturdy ox-drawn carts to the abbey, do not take route D951 which skirts the village and runs along the river, but the main street, going in a straight line between former farm-houses which have now become secondary residences ; there lived the former curser of consciences Maurice Clavel, who sometimes reviled God. The street goes right to the citadel, then becomes a small country road with neither name nor number, hardly discernable on the Michelin map. First you will go ahead without much trouble, your horizon will be blocked, our rock is covered with evergreen, furrowed with paths where hardly anybody dares go any more. Between wheat fields or sunflowers higher than you, you will feel somewhat lost. Courage.

Raise yourself. Plough on towards our beauty, escorted only by old lonely ravens, or perhaps higher, by a buzzard with motionless wings. When you draw near, there will be flocks of black-feathered crows and jackdaws, with smoke-grey collars and blue eyes, holding the premises. You are being watched from everywhere. You will stop for a moment, your heart throbbing, totally enraptured.

This side of our town is, from top to bottom, sparkling with light and inhabited by cooing turtle-doves. Smitten as you are by the silence, what surrounds you dives on you, escorts you and forces you to ask yourself if you are not some unknown knight, perhaps a prince who has unknowingly climbed the steep slope of Sleeping Beauty's Castle. Treading breathlessly along the last abrupt path, you throw yourself on what is perhaps a curtain or a demilune : it is the *Porte Neuve* (New Gate), with its embrasures, its loop-holes and its protruding stones carved to look like the faces of archers, lions, bulldogs and wolves. A last little climb and you are in a long lane bordered with linden trees and full of mystery, on the North watch-path. The moment has come, at that little distance, to start your courting with gallant words : « *My love, my beauty, my fair one…* »

There you are…

One can also get there by the South watch-path. It starts from the foot of Romain Rolland's house and from what was once and might become again Jean-Christophe's Center, rises slowly among the ruins of the ramparts, the indiscreet sides of the terraces and gardens. The vineyards on the slopes produce a dry white wine. In autumn, you will be able to munch on a few nuts from the walnut trees planted up to the foot of the basilica by a delicate, caring mayor. In short, be it from this side or from the streets, tantalized by bottles from here or there, appetizing odours, precious materials, or dreaming in front of the paintings of the great Hosotte, or those of a secretive lesser known artist, Claude Stassart-Springer, or else of apprentice painters or even naïve ones, keep on climbing from the front or the rear, until suddenly… you are there.

A façade gnawed throughout the centuries, where not one figure remains intact : some have lost their heads, others an arm, others their busts. The monument is eaten up by the sun, darkened by the rain, a Romanesque temple with few narrow apertures, a light flooded chancel split by the large sword-like Gothic arches. At the end of the apse, tapers burn in front of the Virgin who gave birth to God, and in the crypt dug out of the rock itself, a shrine where lie the remains of Lazarus' sister, the saint in love with Christ, a few bits of bones and some colourless hair, mortal remains of an immortal love. Past the transept on the South side stands a full length statue of what our beauty was, rather plain and doleful, so as not to drive the monks into Hell. Such is our queen, apostolic and clerical.

I see her differently.

From one world to another...

Through the only open door, a low and narrow postern where one can only go single file, you might imagine yourself in a space capsule, moving into another capsule through an air-lock. High walls, almost fortifications, surrounded by a gallery with a railing where one could picture angels leaning on their elbows to watch you. Sit for a moment on one of the wooden benches, Sunday-school benches. Behold the tympanum where Christ sits in glory, radiant and trembling with the breath of the Holy Spirit. His hair and the folds of his robe flutter and wave, like those of all who surround him. Lift your eyes above the huge columns which seem to support the towers and the outer façade. We find ourselves in the narthex, which feels like a canal lock ; it is a building which precedes the church ; it was built to shelter the pilgrims and help them become aware of their insignificance before passing from their world into another, sublime one, into the universe represented by the Zodiac signs of the celestial sphere. If the door leaves which shut out the nave are closed, push them slowly and enter with a stately pace. Proceed the way you would to the Holy Sacrament, to the end, from column to column, as though they were the trees of a forest, escorted by the angels and the devils of the capitals, specially the devils, or else monsters, mythical beasts. At the end of the bays, the corolla of a sparkling lily opens. It is the Gothic chancel whose columns have been carved from a block of white stone. Let yourself be lulled and caressed by the faint odour of incense. Then go down into the crypt with veins of blue granite on its walls. There it is where it all began. There our kings knelt. Light a candle if your heart tells you to. The gold of the shrine gently glows.

A vessel on the sea...

The wind blows on the terrace. The old chestnut-trees, so often pruned, still resist its push with a muffled growl. Only a few shaky walls remain. The glorious abbey has disappeared, along with the mansion built by one of their proud abbots for himself, with the offerings of the faithful. The Revolution destroyed everything. This mansion and the abbey became property of the State, and all the stones were sold just like at Cluny, except for the heavier ones, and here we are, contrary to spot height 318, looking to the East, the North and the South because the West is blocked by Saint-Michael's tower. From there, one surveys the same blue earth : hills and forests intermingled, each with its brook, its river, its rivulet. All these ripples of oak-trees, all these wisps of fog unfold in the same direction, first towards the rivers Cure or Cousin, then towards the river Yonne, more towards the North, which has flown along, around or through cliffs. In this domain, from the time of cave men, one seems to be at the centre of our planet, just before it became a flaming ball. If someone said that there was a sea behind, you would believe it. If someone said that there was a bay behind the Eastern escarpments, you would see prows of Chinese junks through the vines, at a distance where sails can be confused with butterfly wings.

At a corner of the terrace wall, there is, as for a historic belvedere, a viewpoint indicator, which is free, and binoculars, which are not, as well as a machine to garble French, German or English. According to Claudel, it is in this tangle that Lazarus and Mary-Magdalene's boat ran aground. The craft has disappeared, but the wind dashes on to the prow of the basilica, and, along each side as into a bottle-neck, spews a violent foam. Big black birds drift along the air currents, then find their shelter in the frieze. Storms crash there with frightful clamours.

Inscribed in a heart-beat...

Many chroniclers, analysts and memorialists have related how the abbeys founded by Girart de Vienne were fused into one, for men, at Vézelay, a little before 864. It is a period about which historians themselves have difficulty not making mistakes.

Girart de Vienne is concerned with his salvation. His wife Berthe is very pious. I have read somewhere that she promised the monks to continue to help them if they dedicated their church to Saint Mary-Magdalene. Would Berthe have had a guilty conscience about her loyalty to her husband ?

Thus the place took the name of Magdalene, more through the inspiration of a woman than by the intrigues of an abbot anxious for celebrity. Thus in their mystique, a few monks decided to cherish there, in their monastery, in the crypt which was their first oratory, the relics of Magdalene, saint and apostle, thought to have come from Palestine with her brother Lazarus, and whose body may well rest there, or, as some maintain, in a grotto in the Sainte-Baume mountain range. Perhaps, some whisper, scoundrels among the monks kidnapped the sacred relics in order to worship them better, and brought them here. We even know the name of their leader : Badilon. Historians claim that he has never existed. However, nothing was impossible at that time for this former courtesan at King Herod's court who, seeing Christ, was smitten with love and remained so for the rest of her life. A dazzling beauty with lots of sex-appeal ! A woman who obtained by her tears the resurrection of her brother !

Historians insist on seeing and touching before drawing conclusions and stating that what is true is indeed true. One has to refer to them so as not to lose oneself in arguments, in disputes, not to speak of anathemas and excommunications. Sometimes, when they are unable to explain, they make up stories, and what they say becomes historical gospel, that is to say gospel truth. Their truth is not all. The supernatural exists. Prompted or inspired by God knows what, men sometimes indulge in daring pronouncements which change the course of events. What no historian can explain results from men's personalities, sequences of things, from what happens in what is nowhere inscribed, except in a furtive heartbeat.

Witches' love-dance...

The original church was the first to burn. Twelve hundred pilgrims perished, rumour has it, in the fire, that broke out on the eve of July 22, 1120, Saint-Magdalene's Day. The church was rebuilt as a more grandiose structure, in close conformity with the science of astronomy. Every June 24, on the summer solstice, the sun, if not clouded over, hits the exact centre of the middle slab of the floor of the nave, at twelve noon, Greenwich Mean Time, and, from solstice to solstice, from equinox to equinox, the sun lights all the inside stones. If, stirred by passion, you decide never to leave our sacred place, and if you are there on time, you will see the narthex, a little before Christmas, blood-red with the hues of dawn. One might almost imagine that a computer from NASA assisted the architects of the year 1000 to align their sextants. The architectural marvel : we have it. According to Viollet-le-Duc, the basilica is the most sublime link between Romanesque and Gothic styles.

It is not the sky and its summer clouds that make the roofs and towers of Vézelay glisten : it is Vézelay that holds up the sky and the stars. Is it true ? Is it false ? Who can say why another lover rests there in the graveyard and one who had nothing in common with Vézelay or with Mary-Magdalene, except that she could not do without men or love ? For her to lie there, in her grave, it took Paul Claudel, the greatest poet of Christendom, on his way back to his position as consul at Foochow, to encounter her, in 1900, almost a century ago, on the bridge of the *Ernest Simons* which was sailing to China. Claudel fell madly in love with this Rosalia Scibor-Rylska, not yet widowed from Francis Vetch nor from John Lintner, but young and dazzling, who boarded the liner at the island of Réunion.

Without her, Claudel would have written neither *Partage de Midi* nor *Le Soulier de Satin*. Without her, neither Ysé nor Dona Prouhèze would have existed, these marvellous and immortal representations of womanhood in love poetry and dramatic literature.

Rosalia, along with Magdalene, have changed the rock of Vézelay into a land of fire.

Is it true ? Is it false ? Try to understand how, from China, a wild, sublime soul, after setting half the world on fire, could, like the sun, land among us at Vézelay. Claudel was thirty-two when he crossed her path, and because he was a man of desire, miracle and genius mingled so that Ysé should lie here, among us, with, for sole explanation, a sentence by Claudel inscribed on her grave : *Seule la rose est assez fragile pour exprimer l'éternité… : « Only the rose is sufficiently fragile to express eternity… »* This reality has become a legend. Yes, but there is no altar consecrated to Rosalia.

She only lies in the ground, not far from my friend the poet Max-Pol Fouchet, and the great theologian of sulphurous love, Georges Bataille. Witches' love-dance as well as morning of the resurrection : such is Vézelay.

Henri Petit is missing, another poet madly in love with Vézelay « *an eternal place beaten by the wind* ».

When my turn comes, I'll be there.

If I dared...

There are other roads.

If I dared, I would take you where my strongest feelings are. From the crossroads at Saint-Père, I would invite you to take route D958 towards Corbigny, and go as far as Bazoches ; there you are already in the Nièvre department ; if you like Vauban, who was severe for the inhabitants of the Morvan region, you will be able to admire his castle. Jean-François Barbance, a master in book-binding and interior decoration, has redone the walls of the workshop where the marshal did his planning with ceramics bearing his coat of arms and initials. This is worth the detour. From there, drive down the hill where a herd of cows graze. In the village, which has hardly changed at all, a rustic signboard will lead you to the hamlet of Chalvron. Mount Aubin (362 metres) hovers above you with its very old church. Follow the grassy gravel trail. Leave your car there. It is near by.

All around you, nothing but ploughed fields, wheat, or, after August 15, stubble (*chaumes* in French), from which came the name of Saint-Aubin-des-Chaumes. A vast expanse of hills and woods that the labour of peasants has changed into a royal province, like the whole of Burgundy. Behind you, a tiny sanctuary, almost a chapel, girded with ancient tombstones and freshly dug graves.

You imagine yourself in a wasteland. Two or three country roads used for crop-transport and local pageants lead there. The bell in its frail tiny tower only rings for newly weds, christening and funeral parties ; and the dead are gathered there, lined up or helter-skelter : the older ones take up a lot of space, so the more recent ones have to stay close together. Seated in their midst or just a little distance away, leaning against a railing that has a squeaking gate, produce your shopping-bag, eat a few slices of Morvan salami with a piece of brown bread, uncork your bottle of white wine which could be used as mass-wine. Have a sip and then a second sip to the health of the dead and above all to your own, and still better to the health of your dear wife, for you will have time to catch up with them, scattered as they are, so much as by abandonment as by winters. When the young and sublime prophet went into Galilee, he would stop a moment at the edge of Lake Tiberias, in Magdala, in the beautiful house of Mary, the high-born woman who loved him.

The disciples took advantage of the stop to clink glasses, perhaps with muscatel, a heady wine which I was partial to in my prime. The wine harvested on our slopes, if that is what you drink, has the modest flavour of hawthorn, or perhaps of wild rose or cherry if it comes from Irancy. Sniff it, taste it. The salami will give it a bucolic, humorous flavour, which will evoke Jules Renard, who lived a few leagues away.

The church is closed : it does not matter. But it is a sign that one no longer abandons churches devoid of priest, warden and almost congregation to the mercy of vandals. Religion is disappearing. Censers and chalices can be found in antique-stores. The spirit knows no door, absence makes the heart grow fonder. The sky is striped and criss-crossed with vapour trails of big airplanes, and, higher still, with spider-webs of cirrus clouds. Bazoches castle is almost at your feet. Due North, ten kilometres as the crow flies, the towers of Vézelay shine. Let your thoughts fly towards our sensuous, loving queen. Her sweet-smelling glory can be felt here.

A few crows rise up from the stubble and slowly soar around you. When the wind blows strongly, they shelter beside you. And yet, I won't tell you where the king of oaks is, who is almost four centuries old, and whom I call Zeus. The trampling of visitors would hasten his end. Let's leave him in the middle of his court of young hundred year old beeches.

Ulysses' trumpet...

At the end of the summer or in autumn, at dawn if it is to be a beautiful day, all the valleys are covered in fog. Only summits, hill-top roads and Vézelay can be seen. The sun rises over the foamy rollers of clouds and seems to push them on to the flanks of our rock. When he was still with us, Max-Pol Fouchet, the poet, used to watch them jostle under his windows. Then he would leave his writing-table and walk past my house, mentally greeting me, and he would take the road called Windmill Road because of the windmill that used to stand there, just above the graveyard, as though dead people needed flour. Morning angelus bells used to ring from Saint-Michael's tower and those from the villages of Asquins and Saint-Père, still shrouded in fog, answered them. In his pen, not far from there, Ulysses the donkey, who pricks up his ears at the slightest noise, would bray violently. Max-Pol would say, almost aloud, as if responding to all these sounds : « *I am Hamlet, we are in Elsinore, below the clouds underneath us is the sea…* » Sometimes he felt like picking up a skull, turning it in his hands and questioning it. In order to do that, he would have had to run down the steep hill to the old graveyard, for we have two of them,

and in the older one, the graves are even more dilapidated, almost opened, than at Saint-Aubin-des-Chaumes, harking the call of the last judgment trumpets from the valley of Jehoshaphat. Max-Pol also listened. But the only trumpet sound was Ulysses' monotonous melody, if braying can be termed music. Max-Pol thought that, when his time came, he would feel comfortable there, close to Ysé, Georges Bataille, Maurice Clavel and perhaps me, in the lower section with the old folk.

The order was reversed ; now I wonder about him. Does he still think of us ? Does he converse with these ladies and gentlemen ? Does his spirit float light-years from us, on a star that astronomers have not yet discovered, or else has it returned to the vacuum, the nothingness where we were before birth, not caring two hoots for people, worlds, endless time as well as infinity not bound by time ?

Do not tell me that the universe comes from nothing, or that the complex system of life in man, of the pistil in the flower, has emerged from nothingness. It is a mystery. Not to mention love, by which we have all been tormented for better or for worse... Will our beloved Magdalene be there to guide us through a difficult path ? And also Ysé, in whom each of us sees a different face, with a crown of burning words ? Max-Pol would also say : « *Vézelay is a land of memories...* ». To which Henri Petit would add : « *of my highest destiny* ». There are places endowed with such a gift.

We come here to listen to the wind which carries us away into the world of Legend.